Dear Parent:
Your child's love of reading starts here!

Every child learns to read in a different way and at his or her own speed. You can help your young reader improve and become more confident by encouraging his or her own interests and abilities. You can also guide your child's spiritual development by reading stories with biblical values and Bible stories, like I Can Read! books published by Zonderkidz. From books your child reads with you to the first books he or she reads alone, there are I Can Read! books for every stage of reading:

SHARED READING
Basic language, word repetition, and whimsical illustrations, ideal for sharing with your emergent reader.

BEGINNING READING
Short sentences, familiar words, and simple concepts for children eager to read on their own.

READING WITH HELP
Engaging stories, longer sentences, and language play for developing readers.

READING ALONE
Complex plots, challenging vocabulary, and high-interest topics for the independent reader.

ADVANCED READING
Short paragraphs, chapters, and exciting themes for the perfect bridge to chapter books.

I Can Read! books have introduced children to the joy of reading since 1957. Featuring award-winning authors and illustrators and a fabulous cast of beloved characters, I Can Read! books set the standard for beginning readers.

A lifetime of discovery begins with the magical words *"I Can Read!"*

Visit www.icanread.com for information on enriching your child's reading experience.
Visit www.zonderkidz.com for more Zonderkidz I Can Read! titles.

Work at everything you do with all your heart.
—*Colossians 3:23*

Mud Pie Annie
Copyright © 2001, 2008 by Sue Buchanan and Dana Shafer
Illustrations copyright © 2001 by Joy Allen

Requests for information should be addressed to:
Zonderkidz, Grand Rapids, Michigan 49530

Library of Congress Cataloging-in-Publication Data

Buchanan, Sue.
    Mud Pie Annie / story by Sue Buchanan and Dana Shafer ; pictures by Joy Allen.
      p. cm. -- (I can read! Level 1)
    Summary: Mud Pie Annie is a spunky little girl with an exceptional talent for cooking with flair, creating her concoctions with mud, dirt, and a lot of pride and care.
    ISBN-13: 978-0-310-71572-6 (softcover)
    ISBN-10: 0-310-71572-5 (softcover)
    [1. Creative ability--Fiction. 2. Self-realization--Fiction. 3. Mud--Fiction. 4. Christian life--Fiction. 5. Stories in rhyme.] I. Shafer, Dana. II. Allen, Joy, ill. III. Title.
    PZ8.3.B8455Mu 2008
    [E]--dc22
                                      2007023106

Zonderkidz is a trademark of Zondervan.

Art Direction: Jody Langley
Cover Design: Sarah Molegraaf

Printed in China

08 09 10 • 4 3 2 1

Mud Pie Annie

story by Sue Buchanan
and Dana Shafer

pictures by Joy Allen

Mud Pie Annie was a good cook.

She used bowls and spoons and pots.

She marched out with a smile
right to her sunny spot.

5

"It takes a lot of water,"

said Annie as she mixed.

"To make the finest mud,
I use fresh dirt and sticks."

Annie put in some berries
and crunchy leaves and roots.

"My mud will be the richest

when I add green grassy shoots."

Oh, what a feast!

Oh, what a meal!

Annie licked her lips.

She topped her zesty mud pie
with flowers and rose hips.

Mud Pie Annie was ready to share
her colorful homemade treat.

Her tasty fudge from sloppy sludge
would be a treat to eat.

Annie couldn't help herself.

She loved her sloppy paste.

After all that muddy fun,

she had to have a taste.

Then Annie called her friends.

"Come and taste my treats!"

Her friends peeked in her yard,

afraid of what they'd meet.

"We just ate,"

the friends called out

when they saw the runny goo.

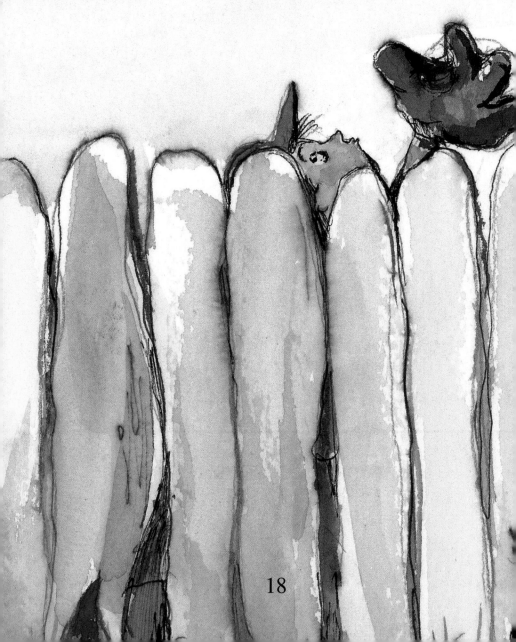

"We'd like to try your food,

but we have other things to do."

Annie's mom and dad came out.

They said that they would try.

They took a look and ran away

from Annie's muddy pie.

Dad said, "Ann is a little dirty.

She could use a good hot bath.

Let's carry her to the bathtub,

or she'll make a muddy path."

Mom put Annie in the bathtub,
which wasn't very fun.

They cleaned her up and told her,

"Your mud-pie days are done."

But silly Mud Pie Annie
picked up her bowl and spoon.

She started mixing bubbles.

They almost reached the moon.

"If I make mud pies," Annie sang,

"or dishes for a queen,

I'll always do my best,

for there is no in between."

Annie wanted to do her best
because everybody knows,

"God sees what's in my heart,

not the mud between my toes!"